THE M

D0537505

"*The Magic Boatho* ho get their just desserts a. ... . o. a ...uly ghost... Arthur Robins' illustrations add a wickedly grotesque flavour to the story... A good read for beginners." *Books for Keeps*

Sam Llewellyn loves the sea. A keen and experienced sailor, he was born in the Isles of Scilly and brought up on the north coast of Norfolk. He now lives with his wife Karen and two sons, Willie and Martin, in the Welsh Marches – except when they are at sea in their ketch, *Loon*, or watching seals, dolphins and stags on the remote west coast of Scotland. He has written several adult thrillers set in the world of sailing, as well as numerous adventures for young people: *Pegleg, Pig in the Middle, The Polecat Café, Wonder Dog* and *The Rope School*.

Arthur Robins has illustrated many children's books, including *Beware Olga!, The Polecat Café, Impossible Parents, Little Rabbit* Foo Foo, *The Magic Bicycle* and *The Finger-eater*.

Books by the same author

The Polecat Café

For older readers

Pegleg

Pig in the Middle

The Rope School

Wonder Dog

SAM LLEWELLYN

THE MAGIC BOATHOUSE

Illustrations by Arthur Robins

WALKER BOOKS
AND SUBSIDIARIES
LONDON · BOSTON · SYDNEY

For
Gabriel
&
Phoebe D.
S.L.

First published 1994 by
Walker Books Ltd, 87 Vauxhall Walk
London SE11 5HJ

This edition published 1995

6 8 10 9 7 5

Text © 1994 Sam Llewellyn
Illustrations © 1994 Arthur Robins

This book has been typeset in Garamond.

Printed in England by Clays Ltd, St Ives plc

British Library Cataloguing in Publication Data
A catalogue record for this book
is available from the British Library.

ISBN 0-7445-3686-3

CONTENTS

FORGOTTEN ORPHANS

The minibus of the School for
Forgotten Orphans was rambling
down a winding lane in the bottom
of a deep valley, crammed with
forgotten orphans heading for their
holiday.

Joe and his sister Doris were at the back, as usual. The Fat Ern mob were at the front, hitting each other. The Soppy Emmer mob were behind them, gooing at their dollies.

The reason Joe and Doris were at the back was that Joe did not like hitting people unless he had to, so Fat Ern's mob said he was soppy. And Doris did not like playing with dolls, or anyway not all the time, so Soppy Emmer's mob said she was fat.

There was plenty of noise in the minibus.

"Shurrup!" roared horrible Mr Barge. He was the driver, and the teacher in charge of the holiday.

The Fat Ern mob shurruped. The Soppy Emmer mob shurruped.

Joe and Doris were so excited they did not even hear.

"You will be punished!" bellowed Mr Barge, who hated Joe and Doris because they were not evil enough and they did not fit in.

The minibus bounced on in silence. The road stopped. Grey waves were bursting on a rocky beach, their spray splattering an ancient cottage.

Joe thought it all looked
extremely interesting, but kept his
mouth shut in case the Fat Ern mob
bashed him one.

Doris thought it all looked lovely,
but kept her mouth shut in case the
Soppy Emmer gang made her
change the nappies on their dollies.

The air was full of the cry of gulls.

Fat Ern turned on his ghetto-blaster.

Soppy Emmer began to sing along. The racket was huge.

The cottage smelt of paraffin. There were three rooms upstairs.

Fat Ern and his mob looked at Joe. "We're not sleepin' with *'im*," they said.

Soppy Emmer and her gang looked at Doris. "We're not sleepin' with *'er*," they said.

"Quite right," yelled Mr Barge. There was a ladder leading to a trapdoor in the ceiling. "You two can sleep up there," he said.

UP YOU GO!

Up there was a small room with a circular window and two rickety beds.

"I like it up here," said Doris.

"Me too," said Joe. "But don't tell them, or they'll change us."

"Right!" roared Mr Barge when they had all unrolled their sleeping bags and were downstairs in the cobwebby sitting-room. "Lovely nature walk next. Except Joe and Doris. Joe and Doris, clean up."

19

"Why?" said Joe.

"Because of not shutting up when *told* to!" yelled Mr Barge.

"That's unfair," said Doris.

"Cheek!" howled Mr Barge, blue in the face. "You're off tomorrow's outing, too. The rest follow me!"

And they filed over the horizon, Fat Ern's mob punching each other, Soppy Emmer's gang plaiting each other's hair.

"Clear up, ho," said Doris. But the cobwebs in the house were thick as knitting.

"Let's start in the garden," said Joe. But the rose bushes were like barbed wire entanglements.

So they walked on to the beach, where they found a boathouse.

"Must belong to the cottage," said Doris. "In we go."

In they went.

There were cobwebs, a mouldy lobster pot and a lot of darkness. And hanging on the wall, a thing that looked like a giant ice-cream cone. Joe unhung it.

"Wrong," said a voice. It was an
old, slow voice. It nearly made Joe
and Doris jump out of their skins.
"It's a foghorn."

As their eyes got used to the
gloom, Doris and Joe saw an old
man.

Then a shadow darkened the
doorway: a fat shadow, with no
neck. It was Fat Ern.

The old man said, "Blow that
horn."

"Blow it yourself, Grandad," said
Fat Ern, whose manners were
diabolical.

"I'll do it," said Joe, whose
manners were fine. He took the
foghorn in his hand. It looked old.
In fact it looked ancient. He walked
outside, on to the beach, and blew.

THE MISTS OF TIME

The horn made a curious sound.
Doris had the idea that it was fading
not so much into the *distance* as
into the *past*. As the last echoes
died, sky and sea turned pearly
grey, and the cliffs and the horizon
disappeared.

"Foghorn," said the old man, cackling. "Brings the fog. And other things."

A noise came out of the fog – a creak and thump, creak and thump, as of many oars. The grey blanket thinned and cleared.

There was a ship in the bay. It had a mast, and oars, and a huge eye painted at its front end.

It swept up to the beach. Men
swarmed down a gangplank.

The old man said, "What do you expect? They're only the Roman Invasion."

One of the Romans clanked up the beach and said something in a foreign language, probably (thought Joe, who owned an excellent encyclopedia) Latin.

"He wants to know for what task you called 'im," said the old man.

Joe thought. "Tidy up the garden, please," he said.

The small soldier clashed his spear across his breastplate.

Orders were shouted.

Someone started a bonfire. In the smoke Joe and Doris could not see exactly what was happening, but it looked like a lot.

In about twenty minutes, the small soldier was back.

"He says the task is finished," said the old man.

The small soldier smiled. Then his dark eyes lit on Fat Ern, and he began to jabber.

"He wants you for a gladiator," said the old man.

Yay! Aw right!

The Roman walked Fat Ern down the beach and up the gangplank. The fog came down again. There was the sound of the oars.

When the fog cleared, the ship was gone.

"That was quick," said Joe.

"I don't call two thousand years partickler quick," said the old man. "Here's the rest of your lot. See you tomorrow."

Even Mr Barge had to admit that Joe and Doris had done a fair job on the garden. But he still would not let them go on the walk to Hot Sands the next day.

"Tidy up the house," he yelled. "You've only done half the job. By the way, where's Ern?"

"He'll be back in time," said Doris, cleverly.

Mr Barge nodded. Ern would not be missed. In fact his mob was looking a lot happier already.

Thug Ed was making a daisy-chain, and Karl the Killer was teaching a kitten to purr.

"Off we go," roared Mr Barge.

Once the file had gone up the hill and over the horizon, Doris and Joe went to the boathouse.

"Nice to see yer," said the old man. "Tidy the 'ouse, is it?"

Doris nodded.

A shadow crossed the open doorway; a soppy shadow, with ten bows in its pigtails. Soppy Emmer.

"I came *back*," said Soppy Emmer. "My shoe got muddy. Look." On her satin ballet pump, there was indeed a speck of earth. The old man pointed at the foghorn. He said, "Blow that 'orn."

"Horrid dirty thing!" said Soppy Emmer. "Blow it yourself!"

I might get a virus!

"Let me," said Doris, who was not fussy. She took the horn in her hand. She walked outside, on to the stony beach, and blew.

A STITCH IN TIME

The horn made its curious sound.
Joe had the idea that it was fading
not so much into the *distance* as
into the *past*. As the last echoes
died, sky and sea turned pearly
grey, and the cliffs and the horizon
disappeared.

"Here they come," said the old man, sniffing.

Doris sniffed too. A powerful smell of cooking was wafting in from the sea. The fog cleared.

There was a ship in the bay. It had a prow like a dragon's head. It shot up to the beach and lay with its sails flapping. People jumped out, and began to wade ashore.

Joe said, "More armour!"

The old man said, "What d'you expect? It's only the Norman Conquest. By the way, there's a tiny catch–"

One of the Norman women trotted up the beach.

She stopped in front of Doris
and said something in a foreign
language, probably (thought
Doris, who shared the excellent
encyclopedia with Joe)
French.

Bonjour, mademoiselle.
Que désirez-vous?

"She wants to know for what task
you called 'er," said the old man.

Doris thought. "Tidy the house,
please," she said.

The Normans streamed up the beach, down the white road and into the cottage. Clouds of dust began billowing from the windows.

Doris and Joe could not see what was happening, but it looked like a lot. In about twenty minutes, a Norman woman was back.

"Says the task is finished," said the old man.

The Norman woman giggled.
Then she saw Emmer. *"Oo la la!"*
she cried, and began to talk with
great excitement.

"Reckons you'll be red 'ot at
needlework," said the old man.
"Wants you to 'elp with that Bayeux
Tapestry."

The Norman lady walked Soppy Emmer down the beach and boosted her on to the ship. The fog came down again.

When it cleared, the ship was gone.

MR BARGE BLOWS IT BADLY

The cobwebs and the dust had
gone too. The cottage was scrubbed
clean, and sweet herbs had been
strewn on the flagstones. Two large
saucepans were bubbling on the
kitchen range, sending out delicious
smells.

"That was quick," said Doris.

"I don't call nine hundred and thirty-seven years partickerly quick," said the old man, pocketing a bottle of wine someone had left on the table. "Here's the rest of your lot. See you tomorrow."

Mr Barge sat down and ate a vast supper. Afterwards, he announced that everyone should play close to the cottage the next day. Then he looked about him as if something was missing.

"Where's Emmer?" he howled.

"She's feeling a bit, er, sew-sew," said Joe, cleverly.

Mr Barge nodded and gulped down another glass of wine. Emmer would not be missed. In fact, her gang were looking a lot happier already. Delicate Daphne was wading around in some mud by the river, and Fragile Fiona was arm wrestling Breakable Bella.

So next morning they all stayed
around the cottage. In the old days,
the air would have been thick with
teases and insults. But with Ern and
Emmer gone, everyone got on
surprisingly well. They even talked
to Joe and Doris.

But Mr Barge mooched around
with his hands in his pockets,
sulking because he had no reason
to shout at anybody.

Then he wandered off in the direction of the boathouse.

"Quick!" said Doris and Joe, both at once. "After him!"

They found Mr Barge standing in front of the old man. He was holding the foghorn.

"That there," the old man was saying, "is a foghorn."

"I know that!" barked Mr Barge.

"It summons fog," said the old man.

"Poppycock!" yelled Mr Barge, delighted to have found someone to shout at. "It is a warning device for seagoing craft in low visibility situations. Look," he bellowed, "one blows it thus." He raised the foghorn to his lips, and blew.

THE KRAKEN LENDS A HAND

The foghorn blared. Joe and
Doris had the feeling that it was
fading not so much into the
distance as *underwater*. As the
last echo died, sky and sea turned
pearly grey and the cliffs and the
horizon disappeared.

DORIS BLOWS IT

The cottage's weedy garden and
snaky paths had gone too. Instead,
a straight road of white stone led
to the front door, beside which a
golden oriole was singing in a
bay tree.

But this time, the echo did not *quite* die. It seemed to hang in the water, and in the rocks underfoot, and to become a huge and awful *bubbling*.

"Here it comes," said the old man, folding his deck-chair.

The fog was cold and full of a powerful smell of rotting fish fingers.

"By the way, there's a tiny catch—"

"What a ghastly smell!" yelled Mr Barge.

The old man was well up the beach now. Joe and Doris held hands. Out in the bay the sea was moiling sluggishly, as if a big paddle were stirring it from below.

But nobody ever knew who Mr Barge thought he was going to complain to. Because a huge tentacle snaked out of the water like the lash of a whip, wrapped itself round his waist and flicked him into a vast mouth that had opened in the bay.

There was a small, watery *crunch*.
And that was that.

"There's no reasoning with that kraken," said the old man. He stretched, and shoved the foghorn down his thigh boot. "Thing you should remember," he said. "That tiny catch. When you blows the foghorn, them from the fog 'as to take one with 'em. I tried to say. Only they kept interruptin'."

The fog came down again.

When it cleared, the water in the bay was still. And the boathouse had gone, and the old man with it. And so had Mr Barge, and of course Fat Ern and Soppy Emmer.

So Joe and Doris
walked back to the other kids
and everyone cheered.
Then they all had a great holiday
which lasted for ever.

PUBLISHER'S NOTE

You have probably noticed some strange words in this book. That's because they are in Latin or French. Here is a list to help you understand what they mean.

LATIN

Salvete cur clamatis?   Hi. Why are you shouting?

Cotta in fossam incidit!   Cotta has fallen into the ditch!

Ferte scalam!   Bring a ladder!

Horta in tres partes divisa est.   The garden is divided into three parts.

FRENCH

Bonjour, mademoiselle. Que désirez-vous?   Hello, miss. Can I help you?

Ugh! Un nid de souris!   Ugh! A mouse's nest!

Eeeah! Cent araignées!   Eek! A hundred spiders!

Oh, les doigts délicats!   Oh, what delicate fingers!

MORE WALKER SPRINTERS
For You to Enjoy

☐ 0-7445-3689-8   *Mary Poggs and the Sunshine*
by Vivian French/Colin West   £3.50

☐ 0-7445-3687-1   *Hector the Rat*
by Tony Wilkinson   £3.50

☐ 0-7445-3664-2   *Gemma and the Beetle People*
by Enid Richemont/Tony Kenyon   £3.50

☐ 0-7445-3665-0   *The Biggest Birthday Card
in the World*
by Alison Morgan/Carolyn Dinan   £3.50

☐ 0-7445-3196-9   *Captain Cranko and the Crybaby*
by Jean Ure/Mick Brownfield   £3.50

☐ 0-7445-3666-9   *Beware the Killer Coat*
by Susan Gates/Josip Lizatovic   £3.50

☐ 0-7445-3668-5   *Impossible Parents*
by Brian Patten/Arthur Robins   £3.50

☐ 0-7445-3667-7   *Taking the Cat's Way Home*
by Jan Mark/Paul Howard   £3.50

Name _____

Address _____

_____